THE FIRE STATION

A Note from
Robert Munsch

A long, long, LONG time ago when I was in first grade, my class had 60 kids in it!

The teacher didn't read any books and neither did the kids. It was not fun.

Well, here is a book that is fun to read for both you and your grown-ups.

READERS RULE!

Before Reading

High-Frequency Words
Practice reading these high-frequency words in the story:

away going too walk

Meet the Characters
Get to know the characters from the story by looking at the pictures and names below:

Sheila

Michael

Firefighter

Michael's mother

Homophones

Homophones are words that sound the same but are spelled differently and have different meanings. **Too** means when something is extra, or also. **To** means going in a specific direction. Look at the sentences below and decide if you should use the word **to** or **too**.

1. Can I come to the park ____?

2. Let's go ____ the park on such a beautiful day!

When Words Sound Like Noises

Blam is used to sound like knocking on the door. *Clang* is used to sound like a fire alarm *Rrrrrrr* is used to sound like a police siren.

Can you think of a different word to describe a loud noise? Think about what a loud action such as running down the stairs, crashing into a wall, hitting a baseball with a bat, or banging pots in the kitchen would sound like as a word.

Phonics

There is an **F** sound at the beginning of the word **fire**.

Can you make an **F** sound?

Pay close attention to the shape of your mouth as you make the sound. It might be helpful to make this sound while you look in a mirror to see the shape your mouth makes.

Try these different activities to help practice the letter **F** sound.

1. Take a close look around you and try to find three objects that start with the same sound.

2. Think of three other words that also start with the same sound. As an extra challenge, can you think of any words that end with an **F** sound?

3. A simple word that has the **F** sound at the beginning is the word **fun**. As you read this word, pay attention to the two other letter sounds in the word.

4. When two words rhyme, they have the same sounds at the end of the word. Take a look at the pictures below and point to any of the words that rhyme with **fun**.

sun   **one**   **balloon**

5. While you read, look out for other **F** sounds at the beginning of a word throughout the story. You can see the sound easily because it will be written in a different color.

THE FIRE STATION

Story by **Robert Munsch**
Art by **Michael Martchenko**

**annick
press**

toronto · berkeley

**To Holly Martchenko,
Toronto, Ontario, and to
Michael Villamore and Sheila
Prescott, Coos Bay, Oregon**

Sheila and Michael were walking down the street.

Sheila said, "Michael, let's go into the fire station."

She knocked on the door:

BLAM - BLAM – BLAM - BLAM

When a firefighter came, Sheila said, "Could you show us the fire station?"

So they went in and looked around.

"Let's get into the enormous

fire truck," said Sheila.

CLANG - CLANG - CLANG -

CLANG - CLANG!

Firefighters came running.

Then they drove away.

Michael and Sheila were

in the backseat.

They came to an enormous fire.

Yucky smoke colored Michael yellow, green, and blue.

It colored Sheila purple, green, and yellow.

When Michael got home, he knocked on the door.

His mother opened it and said, "You can't come in and play with Michael! You're too dirty."

Michael knocked again.

He said, "I went to a fire in the back of a fire truck and yucky smoke got all over me and I WASN'T EVEN SCARED."

Michael went inside and took a very long bath until he got clean.

Sheila came home and
knocked on the door.

Her father opened it and said,
"You can't come in and play
with Sheila! You're too dirty."

Sheila knocked again.

She said, "I went to a fire in the
back of a fire truck and I got all
smoky. I WASN'T EVEN SCARED."

Sheila went inside and

took a very, very long bath.

Then Michael took Sheila on

a walk past the police station.

He told her, "If you ever take

me into another fire truck,

I am going to call the police."

"Police?" yelled Sheila. "Let's

go look at the police car!"

Michael and Sheila got in the back.

A police officer came running. She didn't even see Michael and Sheila in the backseat.

She jumped into the car, turned on the siren, and roared away.

Retell Activity

Look closely at each picture and describe what is happening in your own words giving as much detail as possible.

Friend Meter

Would you want Sheila as a friend? Think about a few different events in the story and whether she was a good friend to Michael.

What makes a good friend? Good friends often listen to our ideas, consider our feelings, are kind to us, and compromise.

After thinking about all the events of the story, where would you put Sheila as a friend? What would make her a better friend?

Create an image of a thermometer or meter that shows good friend, normal friend, bad friend, and poor friend as the different measurements.

Spot the Differences

Look carefully at the two pictures below.
Point to all the differences you can find.

1. Sheila's hand   2. Extra smoke puffs   3. Dad's tie color
4. Dad's hair color   5. Missing bush

Getting Ready for Reading Tips

- Pick a time during the day when you are most excited to read. This could be when you wake up, after a meal, or right before bedtime.

- Create a special space in your home for reading with some blankets and pillows. The inside of a closet, under a table, or under a bed can make the perfect cozy spot.

- Before you start reading, do a quick look at all the pictures and suggest what the story might be about.

- Can you find the part of the story that repeats?

- Can you add actions like claps, stomps, or jumps to match what is being said to make the words come alive?

- Try to use silly voices for the different characters in the story. Think about changing the volume (e.g., loud, soft), the speed you use to say the words (e.g., fast, super slowly), and how you say the words (e.g., like an animal, like a superhero, like someone older or younger).

- What makes this story silly or funny?

- What part(s) of the story would never happen in real life?

Collect them all!

Adapted from the originals for beginner readers and packed with **Classic Munsch** fun!

All **Munsch Early Readers** are level 3, perfect for emergent readers ready for reading by themselves—because

READERS RULE!

Robert Munsch, author of such classics as *The Paper Bag Princess* and *Mortimer,* is one of North America's bestselling authors of children's books. His books have sold over 80 million copies worldwide. Born in Pennsylvania, he now lives in Ontario.

Michael Martchenko is the award-winning illustrator of the Classic Munsch series and many other beloved children's books. He was born north of Paris, France, and moved to Canada when he was seven.

© 2022 Bob Munsch Enterprises Ltd. (text)
© 2022 Michael Martchenko (illustrations)

Original publication:
© 1991 Bob Munsch Enterprises Ltd. (revised text)
© 1983 Bob Munsch Enterprises Ltd. (original text)
© 1983 Michael Martchenko (illustrations)

Designed by Leor Boshi

Thank you to Abby Smart, B.Ed., B.A. (Honors), for her work on the educational exercises and for her expert review.

Annick Press Ltd.
All rights reserved. No part of this work covered by the copyrights hereon may be reproduced or used in any form or by any means—graphic, electronic, or mechanical—without the prior written permission of the publisher.

We acknowledge the support of the Canada Council for the Arts and the Ontario Arts Council, and the participation of the Government of Canada/la participation du gouvernement du Canada for our publishing activities.

Canada | ONTARIO ARTS COUNCIL
CONSEIL DES ARTS DE L'ONTARIO
an Ontario government agency
un organisme du gouvernement de l'Ontario

Library and Archives Canada Cataloguing in Publication

Title: The fire station / story by Robert Munsch ; art by Michael Martchenko.
Names: Munsch, Robert N., 1945- author. | Martchenko, Michael, illustrator.
Description: Series statement: Munsch early readers | Reading level 3: reading with help.
Identifiers: Canadiana (print) 20220170975 | Canadiana (ebook) 20220170983 | ISBN 9781773216560 (hardcover) | ISBN 9781773216461 (softcover) | ISBN 9781773216706 (HTML) | ISBN 9781773216829 (PDF)
Subjects: LCSH: Readers (Primary) | LCGFT: Readers (Publications)
Classification: LCC PE1119.2 .M855 2022 | DDC j428.6/2—dc23

Published in the U.S.A. by Annick Press (U.S.) Ltd.
Distributed in Canada by University of Toronto Press.
Distributed in the U.S.A. by Publishers Group West.

Printed in China

annickpress.com
robertmunsch.com

Also available as an e-book. Please visit annickpress.com/ebooks for more details.